GingerNutz Takes Paris

An Orangutan Conquers Fashion

Michael Roberts

Foreword by Grace Coddington

Published by MW Editions

INTRODUCTION

By Grace Coddington

What GingerNutz and I share—apart from our unmissable hair colour—is our love of fashion. Even during our early modeling days, we both had an eye for style that could transform the most pedestrian outfit.

And where did we develop this? In Paris of course, where the simplest everyday item can reek with chic.

For me, a favourite source of inspiration was the flea market at the Porte de Clignancourt, where all kinds of vintage clothing could be found at bargain prices. However, "flea" being a word that orangutans are not particularly fond of, I never saw GingerNutz rummaging through piles of antique dresses on a French weekend. She was probably far too busy being a muse.

From the get-go the orange primate inspired Paris designers to concoct their boldest creations. Yves Saint-Laurent's 1940s collection? This was apparently inspired by GingerNutz and Paloma Picasso, the painter's daughter, after they cut up some of his canvases to wear as turbans. Not many orangutans would do that. Or hand out backstage fashion tips to Kate, Cara, Kendall, Gigi, et al.

All of which is why we dedicate this book to the city of fashion and say "Vivre la mode! Vivre la GingerNutz!"

PROLOGUE

To be a top model or belle of the ball
It helps to be slender and strikingly tall.
But if you have arms hanging down to the ground
Not many would think great success could be found.
Yet fashion is freaky (and odd and extreme)
A playground for dreamers off chasing their dream
So even when covered in bright orange hair
A primate can shine with her style and her flair.
Modeling well with superb perseverance
And conquering all, never mind her appearance.

GingerNutz, the world's one and only orangutan supermodel, looked out over rainy Place Vendôme from the windows of her luxury suite at the Paris Ritz. It had been yet another exhausting day of fashion show castings, fittings, and run-throughs; another day of richocheting between one famous French fashion house and another to demonstrate just how daintily an ape can negotiate the catwalk.

Unfortunately, this also involved a tremendous amount of posing, which left her, as the French would say, "très fatigué"—too exhausted to stuff herself on the kilos of bananas hauled up to her suite by room service. And with no energy at all for her new favourite form of exercise, a vigorous hour spent swinging from the glittering crystal chandelier hanging above her four-poster bed. So, after adjusting her night mask, she was soon sound asleep . . .

Briiiing! Briiiing! It felt as though she had only just dozed off when her early morning alarm woke GingerNutz up again.

Off she hurried to the bathroom, while the hotel's entire cleaning staff prepared for the waterlogged swamp they were about to confront owing to her habit of eating bananas in her bubble bath—and clogging up the ancient drains with banana skins.

While attempting to make her legs as silky smooth as those of the other models (even though her hair always grew back within minutes), GingerNutz eyed the pile of messages slipped under her door as she slept. Absentmindedly, she then nibbled on a rare rose from the bouquet sent to her by a French designer who hoped she would model his collection exclusively.

She was about to order her favourite breakfast—a three-minute egg with piles of toasted brown bread soldiers—when several maids bustled in carrying even more vases filled with exotic flowers from other designers hoping she would model exclusively for them too. Because practically every person in the fashion world knew by now, whenever GingerNutz appeared wearing a new creation it became an instant "must have."

Meanwhile, the manicurist waited to tend to her nails and the groomer arrived to untangle her coat.

During the very early part of her modeling career, GingerNutz led a far simpler life, doing everything herself, and every day was just another working day for the world's only model orangutan.

After gulping down a jungle-style breakfast of assorted bugs, berries, and vitamin-enriched roots, she would groom herself and make up her own face. She then set off by bus to her appointments—slowly, because she was always dragging a heavy model bag bursting at the seams with everything she might possibly need on a photo shoot . . . Hair curlers. Hairbrushes sturdy enough to dislodge the most immovable bits and pieces entangled in her hair. Makeup in every possible jungle hue. Some pineapples and a coconut or two for a mid-morning snack. Plus tropical flowers and parakeet feathers for decoration.

Fellow bus passengers, recognising the chic orangutan from her numerous billboards scattered about the city, would nudge each other excitedly, as people often do when finding themselves in close proximity to a real live celebrity. And even those who were not dedicated followers of fashion or knew nothing of red carpet events were often caught casting admiring glances at her orange coat.

She kept her appearance neat, her hair unfussy, and watched her diet closely at all times, whether on assignment in London, Paris, or New York. And in time she learned to pack her model bag with only those items strictly necessary. One wire hairbrush, one steel comb, anti-bug spray, and an extra bunch of bananas just in case the shoot ran late. Plus a nice long stick to poke about in holes for insects whenever the photo crew took one of its many coffee breaks.

Occasionally, she might take along a few of her own accessories made from the flotsam and jetsam collected on the Borneo beaches. Items like shell bracelets and seaweed earrings—things that looked pretty enough in a photograph despite their strong seawater smell.

However, being a young orangutan far from home did have its lonely moments. And it was during these that she sat down and quietly made crayon sketches of her travels to send back to her parents.

Sometimes she might even pose for a selfie with her very excitable fellow models. But alas! These lovely girls were not always so lovely. Especially the more competitive ones who wouldn't tell her where or when lunch was being served on photo shoots or gave her completely false directions to the next casting—a trick that led her down many a dark alleyway covered in graffiti on the wrong side of town—scary places even for someone brought up in the deepest, darkest rainforest.

But in her own good-natured way, GingerNutz shrugged off any unpleasantness because being the world's only orangutan supermodel made her feel confident. And unique. For example, while most of the other models' work bags were divided into compartments labeled "safety pins," "sewing kit," "sticky tape," "extra shoes," "hair pieces," and "chicken fillets," hers was divided into "tasty bugs," "yummy worms," "chewy twigs," and "nutritious berries."

FLORE

Glancing at her agenda, GingerNutz could see how hectic the morning was about to become. Her appointments were spread all across the busiest parts of Paris. And on this particular weekday the street markets were open, which meant every boulevard and "petite rue" would be jammed with traffic.

Luckily, on a previous visit to Paris this smartest of simians had devised her own special route. By using the rooftops and swinging from balcony to balcony, she could avoid the unmoving lines of traffic below filled with red-faced taxi drivers shouting the rudest French words at each other.

"Regardez! Regardez! GingerNoootz!" chorused the waiters at the fashionable Cafe de Flore, smiling excitedly in their long white aprons as they laid out lunchtime specials of frogs' legs and snails.

“Oh, la la, c’est GingerNooootz,” smiled the bakers waving fresh baguettes and chocolate cream eclairs, while the greengrocers in their market stalls waved fresh vegetables or legumes.

Although tempted to stop and snack, GingerNutz waved back without pausing. She was eager to reach the first stop of the day, her model agency, to pick up her new model card. This contained photos of her campaigns for four of the very latest perfumes: Eau Please! Eau Dear! Eau No! and Eau Contraire!—each scent heady with the exotic aroma of freshly bathed orangutan.

BOULANGERIE
VINS

Eau Dear
Eau No
Eau Please
Eau Contraire

She was especially pleased her route to the agency took her along the Champs-Élysées, the largest boulevard in Paris. It was lined with trees, so she could easily leap from branch to branch up to the Arc de Triomphe at the end, where she might even stop to admire the view.

But not today. She was soon expected at the workroom of fashion designer Azzedine Alaïa, and he was strictly against all lateness. Arriving promptly at the tiny designer's workplace tucked behind the offices of the mayor of Paris on the banks of the Seine, GingerNutz waited for her fitting.

Mr. Alaïa was meanwhile down in the basement kitchen cooking one of his delicious working lunches. All sorts of appetising smells wafted up to entice GingerNutz, who had deliberately not eaten her second breakfast of boiled eggs and toast soldiers in order to fit into one of the maestro's extremely tight-fitting creations.

An assistant accompanied her up to the design room and helped her squeeze into a new skirt sample (which was a bit like a stretchy bandage, pulling her in tighter and tighter until she could barely breathe).

"What is wrong wiz 'er?" asked the designer, entering the room to see GingerNutz from behind attempting to walk without toppling over.

"I sink she cannot catch 'er breath—she is too excited, no?" said the designer's assistant, giving him a doubtful look.

"Breeze! Breeze in and out you strange little creature," ordered Mr. Alaïa, as "Ping! Ping!" went the stitches in the back of the skirt until the entire creation unraveled, tumbling in a heap around the orangutan's ankles.

Having successfully completed the fitting, Mr. Alaïa escorted GingerNutz to the front door with a happy little skip. “Please remember, ma chêre Mademoiselle Nootz—always dare to be different! J’adore your ginger coat and arms zat reach ze floor! I sink you ’ave ze look parfait for my new collection,” he said, “because each dress will be worn wiz ze vairy, vairy long gloves!”

So GingerNutz waved goodbye with her “vairy, vairy” long arms. “Au revoir ma petite,” Mr. Alaïa beamed fondly as she swung away. “Next time I insist you call me ‘uncle.’ Yes, I would like to be known as a monkey’s uncle from now on.”

GingerNutz excitedly decided to tour a little of Paris instead of stopping for tea and banana sandwiches. She climbed the walls of Notre-Dame Cathedral and a fancy lamppost on the Pont Alexander III to enjoy the view before posing for a modern painter on the banks of the Seine, who apparently thought her eyes would look far better located on the same side of her face.

Later, as she passed the Musèe Rodin, she couldn't resist popping in to look at the statues. One of these, named *The Thinker*, fascinated her, and she stood staring at it for the longest time. Then, on her way out, she whispered in its ear, "I know what you are thinking. You're thinking you want to be a supermodel just like me."

After finding new places to wear souvenirs of the Eiffel Tower, GingerNutz was thrilled to learn she had been booked for fashion shows at Christian Dior, Chanel, Jean-Paul Gaultier, Thierry Mugler, Balenciaga, Chloé, Céline, Comme des Garçons, Lanvin, Paco Rabanne, Dries Van Noten, Azzedine Alaïa, Louis Vuitton, and Yves Saint-Laurent.

In the workroom of Theirry Mugler, a designer with a passion for superheroes and insects, she was squeezed into a hot, uncomfortable rubber costume that made her look like a large ant.

At Vivienne Westwood, she almost broke her neck attempting to walk in the world's most precarious platform shoes.

Over at Paco Rabanne she was transformed into a very 1960s-looking orangutan in a plastic minidress and a blue wig, and at Comme des Garçons the designer Rei Kawakubo studied her seriously before adding intellectual clothes with lumps and bumps to GingerNutz's already curvy figure.

In the studio of Jean-Paul Gaultier, who was planning a retrospective of his all-time favourite creations, the designer personally zipped the orangutan into a dress with a pointy, lethal-looking top previously worn by Madonna. GingerNutz liked Jean-Paul. He was always eager to do something young and fun. But it puzzled her that they kept calling him an "enfant terrible" when he was some distance from being an "enfant" and not particularly terrible.

At Dries Van Noten, the assistants dressed her in some sort of baggy floral pyjamas, despite the fact it wasn't time for bed, and designer Alber Elbaz hid all the models at Lanvin under giant frills and bows, which immediately called for hilarious selfies and Instagram posts.

The House of Chanel, on the other hand, was having a curly-wigged French Revolution moment, including a plywood backdrop of the Bastille and a fully working guillotine at the end of the catwalk. What upset GingerNutz here was that none of the shoes fit her, and the meaner girls suggested the guillotine should be used on her toes.

As soon as she returned to the hotel, GingerNutz found a message from her agency saying French *Vogue* wanted her for an immediate cover shoot wearing a hat. Now, most up-and-coming young models would find this hugely exciting. Not GingerNutz. All she could think of was her first-ever shoot for French *Vogue*. This too involved hats, each decorated with delicious-looking fake fruit and flowers. To her great shame, the hungry primate, unable to stop herself, had gulped them all down within seconds of the stylist laying them out on the accessories table.

Upon entering the French *Vogue* studio this time, GingerNutz was happy to see all the hats were plain, with no appetising features at all. Although she still couldn't help trying on a beret. "Stop!" a voice screamed behind her. "Je détest! Je détest! Je détest les small, 'airy creatures qui touch la mode! Touche pas! Non! Non! Non!" The startled young ape spun around—and came face-to-face with the very same French uber-stylist from her first French *Vogue* shoot.

With skin as tanned as a crocodile handbag and oversize metal bangles jangling like a jailer's keys, the woman shouted loudly into her face, until GingerNutz meekly returned the beret to its rightful place.

"Aaah, I know you," said the stylist menacingly, studying her through narrowed eyes. "You were ze model 'oo ate all my ozzer 'ats!"

"And they were exceptionally delicious," thought GingerNutz.

"Today we will be putting ze 'ats on ze 'ead—not in ze mouth, comprenez?" said the woman threateningly.

The orangutan gave an apologetic smile.

From then on, everything went smoothly. The black and white cover photo made GingerNutz look like a glamorous film star. Even the stylist seemed pleased. “J’ADORE!” she roared, as GingerNutz ran off in a nervous panic.

Soon the most famous photographers of the day were lining up to take her picture. One took photographs of her with two huge elephants at the Cirque d'Hiver, another showed her holding two enormous bunches of balloons outside the Jardin des Tuileries, and yet another shot her in a very tight basque, or corset, at the *Vogue* studios in the Place du Palais-Bourbon.

That night GingerNutz went out on the town to celebrate. She started out merrily playing the accordion on the bohemian streets of Montmartre before attending a show at the Folies Bergère, having been given a front-row ticket by her agency. Knowing her fondness for bananas, they couldn't wait to hear her reaction to Josephine Baker, the musical star whose theme for the show was bananas. And so it was that French TV carried sensational news film that evening of GingerNutz chasing the star around the stage trying to steal the bananas from her skirt.

As GingerNutz exited the theatre, an assistant from the model agency rushed up to escort her to a late run-through at Louis Vuitton. “They have created a special idea just for you,” he said, bundling her into a fast car with dark windows.

When the car finally drew to a halt, the doors opened, and GingerNutz found herself at the foot of the Eiffel Tower with all the important executives from Louis Vuitton lined up to greet her. “Here we go,” said one as they crammed into the lift. On reaching the summit the secret was revealed—they wanted GingerNutz to model the entire Vuitton collection solo atop the Eiffel Tower while executing a modern dance routine.

“It’s nevaire been done before,” said the designer Nicolas Ghesquière dramatically, “because only a really special kind of monkey nut could do it.” However, even the nimble GingerNutz wasn’t capable of changing quickly enough from one outfit to another to carry an entire show on her own. And so was invented the GingerNutz mask, an accessory guaranteed to turn every aspiring model into the hairy supermodel she wished to be.

"GingerNutz, you have been asked to go immediately to the Élysée Palace," the orangutan was told as soon as her Eiffel Tower dress rehearsal was over. Sweeping past the guards at the palace gate, she waved a banana in their faces as they saluted her. And when President Macron gave her a warm hug of greeting on the palace steps, she immediately offered him a bite of her favourite fruit.

"Non, non. It is you who is receiving ze award my dear Mademoiselle Nootz. For your magnifique services to la mode," said the President. "It is my honour to zerefore present you wiz ze newest French medal. Not ze Legion d'Honneur but ze Legion de Banane, Premier Classe."

This, thought GingerNutz, is a very special-looking accessory indeed. (Almost as lovely as those she fashioned herself from bits and pieces found back home on the Borneo beaches.) And after the President of France pinned the medal to her coat, the proud orangutan vowed she would never remove it again.

Although that, as they say, is “anozzer histoire.”

The author has donated a portion of his royalties from the sale of *GingerNutz Takes Paris* to the Orangutan Foundation (www.orangutan.org.uk) in support of the protection of the endangered Bornean and Sumatran Orangutans.

AUTUMN ALBUM

GingerNutz models clothes from the Paris Autumn/Winter 2018 ready-to-wear collections.

Exclusively chosen by Grace Coddington.

Chanel

Chloé

Paco Rabanne

Saint Laurent

Balmain

Balenciaga

Commes des Garçons

Miu Miu

Loewe

Louis Vuitton

GingerNutz Takes Paris: An Orangutan Conquers Fashion
by Michael Roberts

Editors: Takaaki Matsumoto, Amy Wilkins
Managing Editor: Amy Wilkins
Design: Takaaki Matsumoto (Matsumoto Incorporated)
Design Assistant: Robin Brunelle (Matsumoto Incorporated)
Production: Amy Wilkins (Matsumoto Incorporated)

First published by:
MW Editions
127 West 26th Street, New York, NY 10001
www.mweditions.com
info@mweditions.com

The publisher gratefully acknowledges permission granted to reproduce the copyrighted materials in this book. Every effort has been made to contact copyright holders and to obtain their permission for the use of copyrighted material. The publisher apologizes for any errors or omissions in the above list and would be grateful if notified of any corrections that should be incorporated in future reprints or editions of this publication.

Printed and bound by Gorenjski tisk stortive, Slovenia

ISBN: 978-0-9987018-3-7

Library of Congress Control Number: 2018938214

Distribution

D.A.P. / Distributed Art Publishers, Inc.
75 Broad Street, Suite 630
New York, NY 10004
www.artbook.com
eleshowitz@dapinc.com